LEMONE SKY

Having Sex With Aliens

A. A. Waite

Having Sex With Aliens

Are aliens really here? Have you ever mated with one? If they look just like us, how would you know the difference? This is Book One of the Lemone Sky series. The author will take you on a personal journey and explain to you how it all began.

Lemone Sky: having sex with aliens

Available versions of the book.

Paperback ISBN: 979-8-9866998-2-0

eBook ISBN: 979-8-9866998-3-7

Cover Art by Ultrakhan22

www.the-crazy-author.com

We Are Attannania   1

The Gift   9

The 4th Angle of Perception   15

The Interview   21

Male Essence   30

The 5th Dimension   42

Human Disguise   49

It's Complicated   58

Shadow People   69

The Coming War   88

We Are Attannania

The year was 2015, it has been about 3 years since Gideon last opened his Facebook account. He wasn't sure that he would remember the password, but it opened on his first try. He'd made a promise to himself that he would not reactivate his Facebook account until he finishes his degree; Gideon kept this promise. He didn't think it necessary to have a degree to succeed in the line of work that he planned on doing, but he got it anyway as insurance for the future.

I have never seen her before. She arrived with a friend whom I haven't seen either, not since I graduated high school. We talked about the old days, and I asked about old friends, but she hadn't said a word; only my friend and I were talking. I was so surprised to see him that I didn't bother to ask him about her - who she was, where she was from, and who were they dating? He never said anything to me about her.

I tried to put some music on, but the computer wouldn't work, and the lights began flickering.

"Can I come in?" She asked me.

"Ya sure, come on in," I told her, but my friend Dennis refused to come inside. He said that he'd rather stay outside by the door where it was warm, which I found very odd for him to say, for it was quite hot outside. But I said ok.

The lights flickered and went off as soon as she walked in. I tried to turn them back on when she entered the room, but the lights wouldn't work.

"That's weird," I said, "I don't know what's going on."

She didn't speak at all. She just stared at me while I flickered the light switch; at which point, I gave up on the light and tried once more to get some music going. But the lights didn't work and neither did the computer. She voluntarily unhooked the computer cables, untangled the chords, and handed the laptop computer to Dennis without saying a word. He took the laptop from her and immediately went to work on it to try and fix it, I guess. I remember Dennis being very much up to date with all sorts of technology in high school, so I didn't say a word; I just let him have at it. I began messing with the light switch once more trying to see if I could get lucky and avoid her penetrative gaze; for I was a bit anxious. But the lights still wouldn't work.

At this point, we were alone in the dimly lighted room, and I remember how I'd braced myself with anticipation and excitement; for I was delirious, while at the same time very eager to know what was going to happen next. She was standing in the doorway looking at me, while I was sitting on the bed. And that's when I realized that something was planned.

I could tell that she was very much into me because as I sat there on the bed and she kept looking at me, I sensed this feeling of connectedness that was there in both of our eyes. I don't remember what we talked about, or if I'd asked her anything; I may have asked her for her name, where she was from, and such. Although I don't know exactly; for I don't remember her answering me at all, at least not until after what she did to me, and she was getting ready to leave.

I remember being aroused by her presence. I had only thought of her sitting on the bed next to me and caressing me, but this triggered a chemical release of nitric oxide into the arteries of my copulatory organ. And then all of a sudden, she started to vanish from before me. I could no longer see her true figure, just an ethereal reflection of her body, as she gradually vanished into the thin air. She became like a translucent light and started glowing, and I could see right through her body.

I watched as she walked gracefully toward me. I tried not to panic. I rubbed my eyes and shook my head to get back into consciousness, but she was still this translucent being and she was walking slowly toward me.

She got in front of me; she was standing over me and looking down - reaching in slowly with her head as if she wanted to embrace me. But I was frightened, so I got up from the bed and walked hurriedly towards the lights - trying to turn them on once more, but the lights still wouldn't work. I raced towards the doorway, for the door was still open. I didn't feel her touch me, but something prevented me from getting out of the room. I was reaching for the purple drape that was hanging over the entrance: nothing was holding onto me physically, but I just couldn't move any further.

I knew that she wasn't in front of me, because I couldn't see her, but I sensed that she was standing behind me. I tried reaching for the drape once more, but this time my hands wouldn't move either. I called out for my friend; I shouted for him. "Dennis!" Dennis!"

His eyes were fixed looking down at the computer; he didn't even look towards the doorway - blocked only by the purple drape that was hanging over the entrance of the door. It's as if he wasn't there, or he was ignoring me; unless perhaps, he really couldn't hear me. But I could see him; he was sitting by the right side of the doorway and looking down at the computer.

"Help! Help!" I shouted, hoping that someone would hear me; for I could hear people walking in the hallway. I became certain that they couldn't hear me when suddenly, I realized that I couldn't hear myself shouting. I shouted from the bottom of my lungs: "Help!" but not a single sound came out of my throat. The drape blocked the entrance into the room, so no one could see us inside, but I saw portions of their bodies as they walked by.

I felt her bare skin against mine as if we were already naked, but I still had my clothes on. And then, she whispered something in my ear, "we're giving you a gift," she said, before appearing in her full form in front of me. She looked even more beautiful than before with her naked body against mine. Her face was smooth and glossy, and her eyes gleamed with light; they were brown with shades of purple.

At first, I was on top of her, then she was on top of me, and then I was on top of her again. We were both sweating profusely as if we'd been this way for hours; however, it felt like only about a minute had passed.

She moans periodically in excitement, and I fell in and out of consciousness as I was inside her. I felt the moistness between her thighs, and I wasn't in control of myself anymore. I couldn't tell whether we were standing upright or laying down, for it felt different, like neither: we were floating through the air.

Her skin was brown and fluorescent, it gleamed with light. She became full of the essence of light as I began shaking uncontrollably on top of her. It was the most intense orgasm I've ever had.

As soon as we were finished, she got up from the bed and began gathering her stuff, but she kept her eyes fixed on me while she was putting her clothes on.

I remained stretched out in the bed on my back - and looking up at her getting ready to leave. Part of me wanted her to stay, and the other part of me wondered about this strange encounter: "What just happened to me? Who is she? When did we lay down in this bed? When did we take our clothes off? Why am I sweating so much? Why can't I get up or move? Why was her body fluorescent? How did she disappear and then reappeared like that?" I must've lost track of the time while we were still entangled, because all of a sudden, the room felt quiet and lonely like we were the only ones left in the world.

I thought about calling out for someone to help me once more; for I was paralyzed in my arms and legs. I wanted to call for Dennis, but I didn't make a sound. I was conscious and alert, but I also felt like I didn't want her to leave, for I wanted more of it; whatever it was that she did to me.

She walks casually outside the door to retrieve the computer from Dennis. Dennis handed her the laptop and stood by the doorway looking in at me with a very odd expression on his face. He wasn't happy, nor was he sad; he just peered in at me very strangely, like I wasn't even there; even though I was lying there - naked with an erection in the bed. Although I was embarrassed that he'd seen me like this; I still wanted him to say something, or for him to try and help me.

Whatever just happened between me and her: Dennis had no concern in his eyes about it; it didn't seem to bother him at all. I sensed no threat in his presence, but I began wondering if he was there. "Was that Dennis?" Someone else must've been looking at me from behind those eyes.

She returned the computer to its rightful place, and connected the cables once again. She then turned and said to me: "We are Attannania. We came from 5th dimension. We enjoy very much mating with you. We make a gift for you." And with that, she turned and walked out the door; Dennis followed after her without saying goodbye to me.

Still not able to move, I watched them leave through the side of the drape; for the door had bounced back open after they left. They were walking down the hallway, and then they quickly vanished into thin air right before the door slammed itself shut again.

I look over at the computer; the lights in the room begin flickering, and the computer turns on by itself right after. Some sort of news program was being displayed. I saw soldiers wearing camouflage green pants in big black boots, as they were marching along this rugged terrain that was covered in mud and water; for it was raining. I lay there on the bed looking up at the ceiling for answers, pondering to myself about what had just happened to me.

The Gift

She wore a figure of great elegance - beautifully sophisticated; basically, she had the perfect body, and her skin was soft and warm. Her name too was different, which she shared with me only after she was getting ready to leave. She looked Indo-American of some sort: African American mix with Mexican, Pakistani, or maybe even Japanese. Her breath however wreaked with the smell of fire, like the scent of incense burning. Her breast felt plum and luscious against my chest, and her brown skin glowed with the fluorescence of gold as if she was about to burst into pure light.

"This isn't me. I need to stop this right now. What's going on with me? Why am I even feeling this way about her after what she just did to me? What exactly did she do to me? We just had sex, and that was pretty much it. Or was it?"

Gideon had to stop journaling for just a moment to recollect his thoughts, for he felt an erection coming on while remembering her.

The lights in the room began flickering again; they came on for good this time, and I was finally able to move. I got out of bed, got down on my knees, and began to pray. *"Dear Lord, I ...,"* but that's all I had left in me; that's all I said, for I was not able to find the words. I felt unclean. I felt dirty. I put my head down on the pillow and wept for several minutes.

When I got up from the floor and realized that I was still naked, I walked over and closed the door. I went and took a hot shower, but I was in there for much too long. I didn't feel good about myself. I was in the shower weeping, letting the warm water run down my body as if I was able to wash the stain away, a stain on my soul. After I got out of the shower, I put some new sheets on the bed. I was hungry, but I didn't bother eating anything, for I was too caught up in my thoughts. I curled up under the covers and began weeping once again. As I reflect back: what had happened to me troubled me deeply. I was troubled because I don't know who, or what she was. I didn't know what she did to me.

Gideon set his pen down for a moment because the thought of her body gave him an arousal once more. He sipped some tea from his cup, sat the cup down unto the table farther away from him; he put his elbows on the table, and began gazing into the distance before him; and as if going mad, he started having a conversation with himself.

"*She came to my apartment with Dennis, with just one thing in mind: she wanted to have sex with me.*"

"*But why?*"

"*Could she be an alien who wanted to be inseminated?*"

"Stop the nonsense!"

"Was she a demon?"

"No, I don't think so. She was young and beautiful."

"And was that Dennis? Why did he act so strange towards me?"

"Oh shit! What if she was an angel; one of the bad ones?"

"Yes, that's it! She's a witch, and Dennis was her subject. That explains why he didn't say anything to me when he saw me naked on the bed. Or perhaps he couldn't."

"I don't know; I just don't know," Gideon said, covering his eyes with his hands and rubbing his head, as if the answers would come to him, but they didn't come; they didn't pop out of his head. All he had were unanswered questions and assumptions, and he had no one - aside from himself that he could talk to about it.

He can't imagine himself sharing this information with any of his friends. "I think I got raped by an alien being from another planet. Or, I had sex with an alien from the fifth dimension." Yea, that conversation wouldn't set right with anyone, at least not for people in their right frame of mind. He would be abandoned by his friends; and if they had the right connection, he'd probably end up in a mental asylum.

He hated what she did to him, although he had no real reason why. He could not recall the situation with her without getting himself excited. He loved it, whatever she did to him, but he hated it as well. Perhaps she would've stopped if he'd asked her, but he never did say no to her, and he didn't tell her that he wanted her to stop. However, he also couldn't hear himself shouting, and maybe this was the reason why he never tried saying no to her. But would it have worked? Would she stop if he'd asked her?

Gideon hasn't seen Dennis for the past 10 years; it was strange for him to show up like he did, out of nowhere, and without notice. There were several messages shared between them over Facebook, and in those messages, Dennis acted suspiciously: he was anxious to know where Gideon was staying, where he works, and at what times he'd be home. But Dennis didn't share any information about himself with Gideon, nothing about what he was doing for the past 10 years of his life, or where he'd been living since they graduated high school together. He didn't tell him that he was going to visit him so soon either.

They weren't great friends in high school, but they were acquaintances. He'd asked Gideon for his home address along with his phone number, and Gideon gave them to him, but he had no idea that Dennis would show up at his apartment the next day.

"If she wasn't human, how was her body able to do that?"

"At least I'm ok."

Gideon was ok, but he just couldn't quite fit the pieces together. He had no idea who she was, no idea where she came from, and no idea why she came to him, except for what she told him: that she came from the 5th dimension, her name was Attannania, she spoke in first-person, using "we" instead of "I" as the preferred pronoun to describe herself. And then there was Dennis: he just couldn't get over the way Dennis was acting.

He was too easy, for as soon as she walked into the room; she didn't even share a smile with him just yet, but he was immediately aroused by her presence. She was very attractive, but if she was meant to harm him, things would've turned out very differently.

A few days after his encounter with the transparent being, Gideon started seeing signs, strange things started happening around him. He started hearing strange sounds and seeing things that normal people are not able to do. He could see ethereal energy fields and read the energy chakra (the aura) around people, and he knew when they were pretending.

"She said to him, "we make gift for you." She was trying to tell him that she opened his eyes to see the 4th dimension; for he could see things from a new perspective. Indeed, she gave him a gift. Although he may think it's a curse, that depends; for it's up to him to decide what he wants it to be."

The 4th Angle of Perception

It took him a while to realize his new gift, but when he found out that he had this new gift, he became troubled; for he saw things that frightened him, things that were better left unknown.

He felt as though he'd become enlightened, while cursed at the same time. He couldn't explain why he was able to see the spirit realm (the 4th dimension), and he didn't know how to make it stop. He could see human beings in both their physical and metaphysical forms, and he could see translucent beings (spiritual entities) who aren't visible to others in the physical realm. However, they coexist with humans on the physical plane, although they communicate on different dimensional frequencies.

Think of a colony of ants: any normal person would not be able to hear the ants communicating with each other, but they do communicate with each other using different frequencies in sounds than humans do. It is the same as this with spiritual entities in the spirit realm, who are also 4th-dimensional beings. They exist on the physical plane with humans, but they are colorless, and they operate on different frequencies, and may only be seen from the fourth dimension or higher angles in perception. However, they are merely spiritual entities: pure energy - electromagnetic current, that humans can pass right through them.

Gideon could see electromagnetic waves emanating from the thoughts and emotions of people, which formed luminescent colors of auras around them. He saw how the different spirits are attracted to each other based on the luminescent colors emanating from them.

The upside to his gift is that he could see spiritual entities as they truly are in the final incarnation of themselves: as the essence of light or darkness.

The entity of light carries a core of light that attracts colorful auras, while the entity of darkness carries a core of darkness and attracts pale and colorless auras. There is also a third kind of spirit which is considered neutral or lukewarm since it doesn't have a core of light or darkness; its core is pale and colorless, although its auras are also colorful.

Several days later, after his encounter with the being from the 5th dimension, Gideon drove himself to the park and went for a walk. As he was walking along the trail, he started noticing things; it was as if the whole forest came alive: the birds not only sang to him, but they spoke to him.

"Humans are coming!" they said, chirping at each other. "It's a masculine spirit!" "Let's say hello." "Hello! Hello! Hello! Hello! Hello!" They all said chirping. "Oh well! It's another dumb spirit; it doesn't speak. It doesn't understand us. Leave it alone," the birds said, making chirping sounds.

"I must be going crazy," he said to himself. "Why do I feel as if I understand them when they're just making chirping sounds?"

The trees too were communicating with him and wanted to share their gravitational energy. "Come closer. Touch me. I have what you need to rejuvenate and recalibrate your soul light; my energy waves will give you vitality. I am here to serve you. Come, let me soothe and revitalize your spirit," the trees said, tossing their branches to and fro in the wind showing off how lively they were.

The water flowing from the rock down the stream seems even more energizing. The butterflies, the bees, and all the little critters that made buzzing sounds seemed to be communicating in a way that he could understand. He wanted to communicate with them, but he didn't know how. He just knew that he could understand them. The different frequencies - the sounds they were making meant something to him.

His senses were heightened, mainly his hearing and vision; his other senses remained fairly the same. He could hear sounds selectively and see things on the ethereal plane; he now had a 4th-dimensional view of things, because he was seeing corporeal matter, while at the same time, he was able to see spiritual energy.

Some of the things he'd begun hearing and seeing terrified him because they were ominous things; things that he shouldn't have known.

Gideon despises snakes; he hates seeing them with people. For him: snakes represent evil.

That same day during his walk, he came across a few snakes along the path; upon seeing their ethereal energy, he turned around and walked the other way. He learned that day that snakes are associated with dark energy (dark matter). Every snake he'd seen from that day onward, even the harmless ones, all had the same spiritual core, which could only mean one thing: snakes have an evil essence, or they come from the essence of evil.

He saw plenty of rabbits and squirrels that day as well, but unlike the snakes, theirs was a core of light.

When he was almost near the end of his walk, he noticed a flock of crows hovering above the trees overhead. They seemed to be conspiring about something ominous, something that was about to happen, but he was not interested. But as soon as he'd seen them, he became frightened, because there were so many of them. He'd never seen that many crows before, flying in circles so close by him. And what's worse, he was alone in that neck of the woods in the park that day. He saw a blob of dark energy encircling above the trees where the crows were flying in circles: he ran as fast as he could to get out of the woods.

When he reached his vehicle, the crows were following some 15 to 20 feet behind him. He knew exactly what this meant: something dark and evil was headed his way; something bad was about to happen. These bizarre revelations continued to plague him, and that's why he'd begun journaling.

The Interview

"How are you able to write like this? What makes you so different from other authors? You create these new worlds - and the characters: they all just fit together so well, as if they were real places and real people."

"Well, I see the world for what it is, I see people and things in their true form; that is why I am able to write like this. I just write what I see."

She smiles at him after a short pause, because she was quite shocked by his response.

"Wow, you are quite good at this, aren't you?" she said, "but tell me, what do you mean by writing what you see? Are you saying that the people and places in your stories are real?"

After his encounter with the transparent being, Gideon had begun writing about his experiences. Every day he would journal about the things he had seen and the result of what transpired. He became like a seer - predicting future events just moments before they happen. But even more bizarre, Gideon would recall these asymmetric events and then culminate them into fictional novels. These fictional tensions seemed to have no symmetry with the real world whatsoever; they crescendo into real-life experiences and could turn into global climaxes that may happen in the near future.

He would take the true accounts of what he witnessed and form stories around them, giving them fictional characters and a plot twist to make them more interesting, although not unbelievable to readers. He wanted to warn the people about the metaphysical world and inform them about what could be happening to them in the spiritual realm. He wanted to enlighten them about a very near future: the future of the unconscious mind. The most interesting way for him to do this was through his writing. His books about these fictional tales have become quite popular.

"Yes. There are things in our environment, in our world that most people can't see, but I can see them."

"What do you mean?" The reporter asks.

She smiles at him lightly, acknowledging to herself that he's crazy.

"In my book Lemone Sky, I talk about my experiences with the unseen realm. If you want to have a better understanding of what I mean, I suggest that you go and read my book."

"I will get a copy for myself, but could you give us a little preview? I'm pretty sure that all the people watching this right now would like to know what's in it; why should people read your book?" "You do want people to read your book, right?"

"Yes, you're right. I do want people to read my book; otherwise, I wouldn't have written it."

"Why? Tell us why: can you elaborate a little more on this?"

"Well, I want people to read my books because first of all, I want to make money."

"Well, yes, for sure. Of course you want to make money, we all do. But tell us why: are your books fun to read; are they educational? I mean, I know they're not boring because otherwise, you wouldn't have sold that many copies. But for the people who are watching right now, who haven't read your books: why should they want to own a copy; what's in it for them?"

"I believe that my books are fun and educational, because all of my stories have meaning to them, especially my first book "Lemone Sky". In Lemone Sky, I wrote about my experience with this transparent being, a woman I met from another planet. It was after meeting her that I was able to see these things: that's when I began writing about my experiences."

"Hold on, so you're telling me - including everyone watching right now that you've met some woman from another planet?"

"Yes, that is exactly what I'm saying. She came to me when I had just left college, just after I graduated."

"What did she look like? How did you guys meet? Why did she come to you in particular and not somebody else? Did she have a message? What did she say? What did she sound like? C'mon, give us a little more. You have to explain yourself. Otherwise, the people watching this might think you're crazy. I mean c'mon: a woman from another planet; what did she want?"

"It's all in my book, you have to read the book if you want to know the whole story, I explained it all there."

"What planet was she from? Did she come from Mars, Venus, Jupiter, or the moon; what other planets are there: Uranus? Could she talk? Were you able to understand her?"

"She's from a planet called Lemone, which is billions upon billions of miles away from Earth. In the first chapter of my book, I talked about how we met and what we did. She looks normal, just like other people, and she talks normally too. Well, although not exactly. She spoke in first-person, but she looks pretty much the same as everyone else. After we did what we did, she told me that she'd given me a gift, and that was when I started seeing signs and things. I was able to, ..."

"Hold on, I didn't mean to cut you off, but you said that she gave you a gift? What gift; what was it?"

"I'm not exactly sure how she did it, but I can see the 4th dimensional; I can see things that aren't visible to the human eye, spiritual things."

Just one week after his encounter with the transparent being, Gideon's life turned upside down. His apartment was no longer just his own, and his car had become like public transport: spiritual entities traveled with him, and they didn't even know where he was going. When he told them to get out: they'd act like they can't see him; for they paid no attention to him like they couldn't hear him, or something.

He began seeing non-physical forms, ethereal matter around plants and people, the contrails left behind birds as they fly through the atmosphere; spiritual entities followed him around. The entire universe appeared as a weave-like construction of colorful auras around him, which were all just people, places, and things in spirit form.

The spirit realm should be invincible to the human eye, but Gideon could see that people, places, and things have energy bodies surrounding them: angels, demons, and those already dead - walk about freely with their constituents.

There are constant battles for the possession of souls in the spirit realm. Whenever the living person does something evil, the soul loses some of its light, which means that an evil entity has managed to get a little closer to its end goal. Angelic beings, demons, people who were dying, the living, and the dead, had different energy fields around them.

The influence to do something good and worthwhile comes from good spiritual entities, or angelic beings guarding over the souls of their loved ones to help them regain their strength, and to give them the courage to continue the fight.

However, there are instances where the height of influence from a spiritual entity becomes so great that it causes a total transformation of the soul: the living person becomes overwhelmed by the influences of the entity and begins to exhibit behavioral traits of pure benevolence; or depending on the spirit of influence, they may become excessively malevolent.

Gideon could tell whether a person was good or evil, at least at the moment, by the energy field surrounding them. He could predict the outcome of a situation by the spiritual atmospheric conditions at that moment. For example, if there were too many people experiencing negative emotions (energy in motion) and or exhibiting negative thoughts (producing and projecting negative energy): in that type of environment, everything that can go wrong will go wrong.

Gideon not only had hard luck; he also tended for good fortunes to happen as well. He could predict the weather conditions and tell whenever there was a storm coming, or if it was about to rain, and he would have a solution as well: he would know where to go and what to do. He would always leave the place being targeted just moments before the calamitous event happened.

After having sexual intercourse with the alien being, his pineal gland opened, and his sixth sense was activated; otherwise known as 4th-dimensional vision. This was the gift that the alien being spoke of. Some moments during tantric orgasm (particularly at the point of ejaculation), their essence mingled and flowed throughout their bodies, and the pathway to their soul life opened. During this short but peak moment of ecstasy, he lost consciousness, which made him lose control of himself and exposed the pathway to his soul; which she was able to access. She collects his essence and takes him on a journey through her world. She showed him the state of her planet and her people, her entire life flashed before him in a vision. However, when he awoke, he didn't think much about the vision, for he was focused on what was happening at that moment.

The only downside to his new gift was that he could see all of the negativity around him. Seeing the demonic manifestations in people, and seeing how these evil beings adorned themselves under their human disguises terrified him; even though they couldn't harm him; for they could only communicate at certain spiritual frequencies, such as through spiritual mediums, channeling, divination, seance, and magic.

But imagine what it must feel like being next to a person who has no self-awareness; someone who doesn't know that he's a monster; that person could strike you at any moment without notice, hurting you very badly and leave you in a place that you can not come back from. Then they'll say to you, "I don't know what came over me and made me do it, because that wasn't me. And I promise you, that it won't ever happen again." But it will, because at the core of their being is lying this monster whose appetite for the immoral will only grow stronger.

However, he learned how to control his gift; he can turn his 4th dimension - extra sensory vision on and off whenever he likes. He became aware of this when he met another alien being (a sister of the first being) who taught him more about his gift. This being told him about her sister whom he'd met because she recognized her likeness in him. She told him where they came from, what they wanted, and why they came to him. Gideon thought that he was having a dream, but it all happened for real after she hypnotized him.

Male Essence

He had gone to the church to pray because he was worried about the signs, and the things he was seeing. He didn't know what was happening to him, because he didn't understand his new gift.

He was in the church praying when a young woman dressed as a Catholic nun approached him saying, "Come with me to the garden, we'll talk over everything." Seeing that she was a nun, he got up and followed her.

She saw that he was grieving: he was experiencing guilt and shame, and he was worried and afraid because he didn't know what was happening to him: why was he having these strange visions? Why was he hearing these things?

He followed after her because he wanted someone to talk with, to tell them about the visions he was experiencing.

It was a Wednesday afternoon; no one else was at the church that day. She led him outside into the garden, and they both sat on a bench together. Gideon thought that she might be an angel in disguise because she appeared to him at the right moment when he needed someone to talk with, and her soul was full of light.

She wasted no time with him, for she was there on a short mission. As soon as he began talking about the visions and the things he was experiencing; she hypnotized him. She let him fall into a deep sleep and fed visions into his head to make it appear as if he was dreaming.

He was on a beach somewhere with his friends relaxing and having fun, when suddenly a woman driving a red BMW with the top down: she lost control of her vehicle and crashed it into the loggia of a hotel.

The hotel loggia was on a wooden platform that had several columns connecting it to the main building. It had an overhead deck that was filled with guests; the guests had begun panicking and screaming after the red BMW crashed into one of the wooden columns that held the upper deck.

After running her vehicle head-on into the column of the loggia, the driver lost consciousness and the vehicle skidded out of control. The vehicle kept revving itself and skidding until it made a U-turn while still hugging the column of the loggia, it shook the entire foundation of the loggia.

However, the car didn't stop there; it spun itself around and went back in the direction from where it came. If it wasn't for the sand, the vehicle would've crashed into the building: the car revved slowly ahead leaving two deep trenches where the tires skidded through the sand until it reached the wall of another nearby building.

The driver of the vehicle was unconscious, but her foot was still on the accelerator, which had kept the vehicle revving: it would've climbed up the side of this second building had it not been for Gideon and his friends who came to help. They quickly opened the door of the vehicle and lifted the woman out.

One of his friends entered the vehicle and immediately put the car in the park; the others ran towards the hotel loggia to help those people who were screaming from the deck; which had begun collapsing. Gideon stayed with the woman to make sure that she was okay.

He sat her down on a bench and held her close to his lap. She was awakened immediately after he checked her pulse and had begun comforting her: she was okay.

She didn't sustain any physical damage, and neither was she traumatized, but she must have not been aware of her situation, or any of the damages she had caused, because she began smiling and looking at him bright-eyed.

As if looking into the eyes of her life-long partner, the scene around them suddenly changes. Everything around them stopped moving; it was just the two of them now - quiet and sitting on a bench by the beach, staring into each other's eyes. He could no longer hear or see the commotion happening around them; neither were his friends there anymore, nor anyone else, just the two of them sitting together on a bench, and they were focused on each other.

She smiles beautifully, and her deep-brown eyes sparkled with the rays of the sun. Her hair was dark with soft twisted curls, and her brown skin glowed with the light from the sun. Because of the way she was sitting on the bench, the tightly fitted red dress that she was wearing exposed her inner thigh. She felt familiar and special to him.

She positioned herself on the bench, turning her rear towards his lap, and then slightly pulled her underwear to one side - revealing herself to him. He was already aroused before she did this. Without hesitation, he unzips his trousers and slides his cock in. She moans continuously until they both ejaculated.

When he awoke, the nun that was sitting on the bench next to him was the same woman in his dream. He thought for sure that he had nodded off and had a wet dream about her. He felt embarrassed by this and even apologized to her.

"I must have nodded off just now. I'm sorry," he said apologizing while wondering to himself: "How long was I out for?"

"You are not dreaming; this happened for real. Our people are dying. We have no more male essence. We are the fifth Dimension. Our sister Attannania came to you. We are Assania. We came for the same reason. You are helping us."

Hearing the familiar phrases made his skin crawl and his mind raced. He looked into the eyes of the woman seated on the bench next to him and thought to himself: "Surely, she's just a nun; or am I going crazy?"

In this dream he just had, it was a vision which she gave to him: she was trying to explain the current situation of her planet to him. Although not exactly, because some of the things she revealed to him in the vision had not yet come to pass.

"No, you are not crazy. We can hear your thoughts. You have many questions; we give you answers for understanding. We are not this woman. We came from the planet Lemone. Our people die from no male essence, many women, but no more male child. Our fathers are old; they cannot produce male child. We are many women left on our planet; we came for male essence to produce male child. You help us produce male child. If no more producing male child," she said holding her stomach, "our planet dies."

For a moment he thought to himself: "Wasn't this the same vision that I saw when I was with that other woman?"

He felt sorry for her after hearing the story about her planet, for he was concerned for their situation.

"Why me? Why did they choose me? There are so many men on our planet. Why am I seeing things? Why is this happening to me? Is this woman even real?" he said, questioning himself.

He had only thought about the questions, but she already knew what he was thinking.

"Yes, we are real. You have many questions for us; we answer for you."

Gideon was baffled. "How did she know what I was thinking; can she hear my thoughts?" he said contemplating to himself.

"Yes, we can know your emotions," the woman said, placing her right hand on her chest. "Please, don't have fear for us; we came not to harm you, but that you may help us."

He didn't know why she spoke to him in the first person. Her English was off, but she looks like an American. She said that they came here from a planet called Lemone, which was billions upon billions of miles away from the earth. She could hear his thoughts, and she understood what he wanted to ask before he asked it.

"We came to you for male essence. We give you a gift to protect you. Many male species on your planet, but not many good for male essence; for many have darkness in them."

Gideon became a bit more relaxed because he felt that he was safe around her. He went with her at first because he saw her essence; she was a being of pure light. Her skin kept gleaming brighter and brighter as if she was about to burst into pure light.

"What's this male essence she keeps talking about; what is it?"

"Without male essence, our people die. Male essence is necessary for the life of the universe. No male essence, no life in the universe."

"Is she talking about sperm cells or DNA? There are plenty of men here for that," Gideon thought once more to himself.

"We are not talking of sperm. We talk of the comet nucleus. No comet nucleus, no more planet. Universe explodes. The universe falls," she said, clasping her hands and then pulling them apart to demonstrate what she means by the universe falling apart.

Based on what he understood about physics, which was very little, he assumed that the male essence is like a chip off the old block, and without it, life cannot be maintained or reproduced.

In physics, the nucleus is what holds the protons and electrons together; without it, the physical matter will not stay together. The nucleus is like the magnetic force of our planet. Like electricity, it creates life as it brings different particles and elements together. Without this magnetic force holding everything in place, the planet itself becomes a nuclear weapon: the nucleus explodes - disassembling itself into this endless void that is the universe.

Think of what this would mean for different gravitational bound systems, or galaxies: gasses and particles would collide with each other causing mass explosions and extinction of planet life. Male essence is not just the force that holds everything together, but it also gives life; it coordinates and balances the conductivity between negative and positively charged particles.

That being said, the universe itself is unending (boundless) and there are billions upon billions of planets and galaxies. Her species have traveled billions of miles outside their galaxy, but they still haven't seen an end in sight.

The things she told him made him wonder about the source of God: how was God created? When did the universe begin?

But like us, these beings haven't found the answer yet; they just know that there are other beings out there in the universe who are more advanced and more powerful than them. They believe that all life comes from them. Them: a single being with many life forces within one body.

In essence, this single being who is many persons in the one contains all the knowledge of the universe. They can see from all possible dimensions because they are Alpha and Omega.

"Are you an angel?" Gideon asks. "Do you believe in God?"

"We believe in Elixir of Souls, the beginning for all life, the creator for male essence, the alpha male."

Gideon didn't understand what that had to do with him: why come here from so far away just to have sexual intercourse?

"You are not original male essence, but you came from original male essence. If not come from the original male essence, our people die very fast. If came from original male essence, very good for making male child."

"But there are many other male species here on our planet, why not go with them?"

"They have not come from original male essence. We die for mating with them."

"What do you mean not come from original male essence?"

"Sorry for speaking English, not very good for my understanding. If speak many languages, it will be very good for us for understand each other."

She communicates some 10,000 plus languages, but unfortunately English is her least favorite tongue. She understands English very well, but she was confused by the different context uses and meanings behind the English words.

"I speak only English," Gideon said in reply. "But you're doing fine; I can understand what you're saying. But tell me, what do you mean by not coming from the original male essence?"

"If not come from original male essence, not good for soul life."

"And what do you mean by that; what is soul life?" Gideon asks.

"We live many of us together in one physical body, but not very long if we have no soul life."

"Oh, I think I understand you now," Gideon said. "On your planet, your people exist in both physical and spirit form, right? If all male essence dies, you will only exist as pure energy beings without physical bodies. Am I right?"

"Yes, this is what we mean. We must have original male essence to exist in physical form, but if the essence is not come from the original male essence, no more soul life."

"So, does this soul-life of which you speak, is this what connects you with God, the Elixir of Souls; if you lose this soul life, your connection with the Elixir of Souls will die?"

"Yes, this is what we mean. We must not lose connection with Elixir of Souls. If we lose connection with Elixir of Souls, no more soul life, we all die."

"Are you saying that I have God's DNA inside me?"

"What's this mean DNA?"

"DNA is our gene code. It is our essence; more like what you call comet nucleus."

"Yes, you have the essence of comet nucleus. We too have the essence of the comet nucleus. Together we make child that came from comet nucleus. We are beings of pure light. You too have come from pure light. We came for mating with male species of pure light to give us male essence to make male child. If not come from pure light, much darkness comes in, male child kills people of the universe. Darkness is no good for soul life. If darkness comes into soul life, light from Elixir of Souls goes out, and soul-life dies."

The 5th Dimension

"What is the 5th dimension?" The reporter asks.

"The 5th dimension is like being able to see the body from inside itself, although not exactly."

She looks at him confused.

"Let me try and explain what I mean," said Gideon. "The 4th dimension is like when we're dreaming. We may dream of achieving something impossible, only to be awakened moments later and realize that it's something that didn't happen. Or did it?"

"Sometimes we dream about things that we can't physically do with our bodies. This is because when we dream, we dream in our physical body, but our physical body does not go everywhere that our minds take us, it remains stationed for the most part, for most people. But, our mind can take us wherever we want to go."

"Some people experience dissociative episodes, while others dream of their souls leaving their bodies behind. These out-of-body experiences are considered 4th dimensional; for it is like being outside of the body and being able to see through the body. However, the 5th dimension is like being inside the body and being able to see through the body itself, but you can also see outside of the body as well."

"Let's say for example that you were an orange; inside the orange, you have the seed. The 4th dimension is like being outside of the orange and looking in to see right through it until you can see the orange seed. The 5th dimension is as this: you are not just the orange, but you are also the orange seed. So, because you are both the orange and the orange seed, you would not just be able to see the outside of the orange, you are able to see the inside, and through the orange as well."

"The 6th dimension would be that layer beneath the layer of the orange seed. The 7th dimension would be the layer beneath that layer of the layer beneath the orange seed, and so on and so forth. This goes on until there is a complete breakdown of not just the physical properties of the orange, but also the non-physical properties as well: solid matter is broken down into gasses, or subatomic particles, such as protons and electrons, electromagnetic wave frequencies, and such, until the solid itself dissipates and disassembles its nucleus; which at that stage it becomes as anti-matter."

The reporter looks at him more confused than before. "I'm sorry," she said, "can you explain it to me in layman's terms. I'm sure that the people watching kind of feel the same. I mean, I get what you're saying about the orange seed, but all that other stuff just went, oops!" the reporter said using her hand to demonstrate that the topic went over her head.

Gideon gave it another shot.

"Humans, he said, "are three-dimensional beings. We are able to see the inside and the outside, as well as around objects; sometimes we can see right through them. However, this is only possible when we have a certain freedom of perception: we may adjust the object itself or adjust our angle of perception so that we can see four-dimensional. But even after doing this, there is always that blind spot that we can't see. This blind spot is what causes us to want to change perspective or change the angle of perception to see the object in full view."

"The blind spot will always be there, even for the 5th dimension, 6th dimension, 7th dimension, and so on, all the way through to infinity; although there are truly only seven dimensions, which are known as the seven stages (or seven states) of matter. But if you want to get religious: the seven dimensions are the seven perspectives, or spirits of God."

"The difference between dimensions are the angles of perception, which multiply to an infinite number as the properties may amalgamate and alternate between the different angles of perception and reflect within themselves."

"Amalgamation is when the physical matter is broken down into subatomic particles - from solids to gasses and such, which then converts into electrons, neutrons, and protons (the seven stages of matter). Amalgamation continues until it reaches the nucleus, and then the nucleus itself is broken down as well. The amalgamation process between solid matters and gasses is what creates these infinite number of perspective angles or dimensions."

"Beyond infinity is not impossible, but at the same time, it isn't possible to have a view beyond infinity, because it would be a view from outside of the universe. Even if you are God himself, you would still have that blind spot that you can't see, even after you change perspective or change the angle of the object you're looking at."

"However, there is this theory of an all-seeing eye. The theory of an all-seeing eye only holds if there was a supernatural being possessing such a superpower. This supernatural being is God himself, who can see all things, above all things, below all things, through all things, and beyond all things. God is all-knowing because he has this capability to see things from an infinite number of perspectives, or dimensions."

"When you look into a mirror: let's say you're trying to get your hair done. You will look into the mirror to see the front of your face, but if you wanted to see the back of your head, you would place another mirror behind your head to get a reflection of the view from behind your head. This is how things would appear to someone who has an all-seeing eye."

"But imagine once more that the entire universe is a sphere within a sphere. The outer sphere does not spin, but the inner sphere does, so everything inside the inner sphere appears to be moving in all possible directions - up, down, sideways, perpendicular, parallel to each other, etc. However, the truth of the matter is that all the objects within the inner sphere are stationary; it's just the inner sphere that spins. This outer sphere that does not spin would be like a mirror, and this mirror is being held by God."

"God possesses this all-seeing eye, because he has this mirror, but not just the one mirror, but an infinite number of mirrors, of which he positioned them in such a way that he is able to view the entire universe (the whole of this inner sphere) from a single perspective. God is this all-knowing supernatural being because he possesses this capability to see all the objects within the inner sphere without having to move the sphere or change his angle of perception."

"But the more intriguing question is: what causes the inner sphere to move?"

"Ok then," the reporter said sarcastically, not understanding a word he just said, "tell us who and what are fifth-dimensional beings, how are they different from us?"

"Fifth-dimensional beings are spiritual beings, but they can merge and alternate between the corporeal and incorporeal. They can take on the properties of molecules and become subatomic particles - protons and electrons; so, they may disintegrate completely to amalgamate with the physical matter or other properties available in their environment. They can alternate between physical and non-physical forms."

Human Disguise

It was a very warm Saturday afternoon, and Gideon went grocery shopping. He pulled his car up to the gas pump in the Kroger parking lot and was getting ready to refill his tank. As soon as he started the meter, a German-camouflage Cherokee jeep pulled up beside him on the opposite side; a young teenage girl stepped out of the vehicle, looked at him, and began walking back and forth from her vehicle to the pump, and again from the pump to the passenger side of the vehicle. As if confused, she seems to have forgotten something. She kept forgetting it because she did this several times.

She put the nozzle inside the tank, and began pushing the buttons; and then, she squeezed the trigger, but the gas wasn't flowing.

"Hi, how are you doing?" Gideon greeted her.

"I'm doing fine," she said. "I just got my license today, and I'm so excited."

"Oh, really?" he remarked.

"You've just got your license? I better watch out for you on the road then," Gideon said jokingly, "You might run me over."

"What! You don't know what you're talking about. I'm a good driver," she said sheepishly.

"I'm just kidding," Gideon replied.

After he said this, there was a tense moment between them, which made Gideon feel awkward. They stood by the pump facing each other and said nothing. By the expression on their faces, it was clear that they were interested in each other; they were sending and receiving each other's sensual energy. The sexual tension between them was so intense that you could almost cut it with a knife.

She seemed so childish and unworldly, like a greenhorn – and she wanted to let loose and have some fun. He wanted to be the one who taught this fledgling how to fly, but he was lost for words. He hadn't planned his approach beforehand; he had just randomly provoked her.

She started typing something on her cellphone to try and ease the awkwardness.

Gideon's tank was now full. He put the pump back into its place, printed his receipt, opened his car door and got in. But before driving off, he rolled down the window and said, "It was nice meeting you. I hope you find something fun to do today."

Immediately after he said this, there was a look of disappointment on her face. She didn't reply to him; she just stood there and stared at him - watching him drive away. He couldn't tell if she was vexed, because she had a crooked smile on her face. He watched her in his rear-view mirror, and he noticed her eyes watching him as he left – with a Mona Lisa grimace on her face.

He stopped the car at the bottom of the parking lot, just a few feet away from where he had left her. He could still see her eyes watching him in his rear-view mirror. Normally when he went grocery shopping, he would park closer to the storefront to have the shortest walking distance back to his vehicle. However, this time it was different.

Like shooting game from a distance, and then going to fetch it, she'd kept her eyes on him until he came to a stop. He waited for a moment before getting out of the vehicle. He was contemplating what else he could've said to her, and how easy it would've been if he'd just asked her for her number.

He opened the door and was about to get out of the vehicle, when suddenly the Cherokee jeep pulled up beside him; it was the pretty young thing once again. She was talking to someone on her cellphone. Gideon could hear her side of the conversation because she was talking very loudly - shouting at the person on the other end, as if trying to give him clues that she was in control of her situation, and that she was free to do whatever she wanted.

"I'm not ready to go home yet. I'm trying to find something fun to do first. I think I'm just going to drive around town for a while before I come home," she said. She then mumbled a few more words and hung up the phone. Gideon stood between his vehicle and hers and waited for her to finish the call. She lowered the phone from her ear and began pushing the buttons on the screen; she was looking straight ahead and not at him, but in her peripheral view she could see that he was standing there waiting for her to finish the call.

The temperature outside was about 90 degrees; after standing there for only a short while, Gideon had begun sweating.

"So, it's you again huh!" Gideon said.

"What?!" she replied, glancing at him, pretending to be preoccupied with her cellphone.

"Where are you trying to go?" he asked her. The window was already lowered when she had pulled up next to him.

"I don't know, I'm just bored," she replied. "Plus, it's the weekend and I want to do something fun."

"What's your name?" Gideon asked her.

"Nikki," she replied without elaborating. She pretended not to be interested in what he was asking and continued looking down at her phone.

"How old are you?"

"How old do you think I am?" she retorted.

"I don't know, you look quite young."

"I'm 18, I wouldn't be driving if I wasn't," she snapped at him.

"You could be 16 and driving, and you did say that you just got your license?" replied Gideon.

"I'm 18, do you want to see my ID?" she said abruptly.

She reached into her purse and waved her identification at him; he quickly glanced at it to verify her age, and then handed it back to her. She so willingly showed it to him, and she was already getting agitated.

"And it's not fake either, I just got it like two days ago," she said.

"What's your number?" Gideon asked.

"Why do you want my number? I'm not giving you my number, we've only just met," she said, smiling.

"Well, since you're bored, I was going to text you and see if you want to come to my place and hang out later."

"Where do you live, like how far do you live from here? Give me your number and I'll text you?" she said.

"I live up the road. Do you know where the college suites are? I live right there."

"Okay, what's your number?"

She typed his number into her cellphone, and then said, "Like, what are we going to do when we get to your place? Because I don't have much time; I was going to go home soon anyway."

"I don't know; just chill, I guess. We can do whatever you want."

She said nothing.

"Do you want to follow me back to my apartment? I live close by; I mean literally just five minutes away."

They pulled into the parking lot of the apartment complex. Gideon quickly got out of his vehicle and went over to her. "Park over there in the visitor's spot. I don't want you to get towed," he told her.

He opened the door to his apartment and walked in, ahead of her, to open the door to his bedroom. But after opening the door to his bedroom, he turned around and noticed that she was still standing outside the apartment – and the door was slowly closing in her face. He quickly ran back to catch the door, but he was too late – it closed in her face. He opened the door and asked her to come in. She looked to her left and to her right before stepping inside.

He closed the door, and she walked into the living room, towards the open door of his bedroom. She stopped and just stood there. He rumbled around the kitchen and waited for her to walk into his bedroom to use the bathroom or something, but she didn't; she just stood there playing with her cellphone – nonchalantly and spontaneously observing everything in the apartment.

"Do you have a roommate?" she asked.

"It's a three-bedroom apartment, but I live here by myself right now. I'll be getting roommates pretty soon, probably in about a month or so."

He went into his bedroom and left the door open for her to come in, but once again, she waited until he invited her in.

"You can come in," he said.

She walked in and voluntarily closed the door behind them. He used his cellphone to snap a quick photo of her, without her noticing.

She went straight into the bathroom, without asking his permission. When she returned, he was sitting on the bed waiting with his cellphone in hand, and he immediately snapped a few pictures of her. She was completely naked; Gideon hadn't expected to see her like this so soon.

She launched herself at him and wrestled the phone from his hand. She deleted all the pictures of herself, except the one that he had taken earlier when she had clothes on. She handed the phone back to him and went back into the bathroom. He waited a moment before following her.

She wasn't upset; if anything, she was a little concerned about what she'd done: when she launched herself at him - she was incredibly quick and strong, but Gideon didn't seem to notice anything unusual about her; except for the fact that she was naked.

It's Complicated

He stood behind her and put his arm around her waist. He stared at her in the mirror – examining her naked body for blemishes. Her eyes were looking down instead of looking back at him. He raised his hands to touch her auburn hair, and then he lightly grasped her melon-size breasts. He then reached both hands down and touched the front of her vagina. She didn't flinch or say anything, she just let him.

The red sweater and the tightly fitted jeans that she had worn were lying next to her handbag on the bathroom floor. They didn't look like they were carefully placed; she had taken them off in a hurry and had tossed them on the floor.

"Why didn't you want me to take your picture?" Gideon asked, looking at her in the mirror.

"Because," she said.

"Because what?" he asked.

"Because, I'm naked and plus my hair is a mess."

"You still look pretty, though," he said, complimenting her while still tracing his hands over her body.

She smiled at him in the mirror once again with that Mona Lisa grin. Her eyes glanced at him to see where he was focusing, but only momentarily; she was mainly looking down, as if trying not to make direct eye-contact with him.

He told her that he wouldn't take any more pictures, and then started to undress himself as he stood behind her. She watched him in the mirror. He pulled his shirt up over his head; his stomach flat and chiseled, his chest and muscled arms glowed with sweat. He unbuckled his pants and tossed his clothes onto the bedroom floor. He embraced her, leaning her against the sink. Her melon-size breasts stood lusciously in the mirror in front of him as he forced his shaft between her legs - letting it rub against her clitoris. He stopped and waited for her to react: for her to ask him if he had a condom, or say something, but she didn't. Instead, she pivoted her body against him and began twisting and turning - gyrating against him, trying to get him inside her.

He pulled himself back. "Hold on," he said, and went into the bedroom to get a condom from the chest drawers. When he returned, he held her from behind and placed the unopened condom on the sink in front of her.

She looked at it and glanced up at him from behind the mirror. "I don't want to use a condom," she said.

This caught Gideon by surprise. She noticed the skepticism in his eyes, and his reaction: he stopped rubbing against her and loosened his embrace.

"You're okay, but I've had bigger than you before," she said, as if this was supposed to make him feel better or make him lower his defenses. But instead, he felt indifferent toward her; he was no longer interested in having sexual intercourse with her.

Men like it when women are spontaneous and promiscuous, because this simplifies things for them. If she lets him in right away, this means that there's instant connection between them. Men don't like beating around the bush; they rather get straight to the point, even though most men won't willingly admit this, or say this to a woman the first time meeting her. But if she's easy and promiscuous, can she still be as good?

This flash of promiscuousness and spontaneity is the ideal situation for a man to be in with a woman whom he desires to have sexual intercourse, because most men would rather not have to prove themselves before getting what they want from a woman. It doesn't matter if she's unchaste, if he enjoys his time with her, he may even divorce his wife to marry her.

Samson was betrayed by a promiscuous woman called Delilah; David and Solomon had many concubines; Jesus allowed a promiscuous woman to kiss his feet and then dry them with her hair. Women who are promiscuous acts with spontaneity; this implies a sense of freedom and independence: that she can carouse without limitation or concern, because she has nothing to worry about.

However, hearing the words she confessed shocked him. She said the one thing that she thought would have motivated him and caused him to make his move on her; for she noticed how spontaneous he was as well. But instead, he was turned off by what she said.

Gideon now had two options in mind. One, ram his cock inside her to prove his masculinity: he could be just as good as any man she's ever had, or better; for he was angry, and this made him want to go wild with her. Two, he was concerned about getting her pregnant.

"I won't get pregnant," she told him, "I'm on birth control."

"But still …," he said to her.

"I'm clean, if that's what you're worried about," she said, glancing up at him in the mirror.

"I mean, we just met though," he said, letting go of her and walking back into the bedroom.

He sat on the bed and waited several minutes for her to come out of the bathroom. He was turned off by her comment, but she was a pretty girl. He wanted to try to at least please her, to give her some form of pleasure for having come this far to be with him, and for having trusted him – a complete stranger. He hadn't had sex in many years; except for last night, the morning after - when he awoke with that naked girl in his bed. She had sex with him during the night while he was fast asleep, and she had squirted all over his bed and lied to him when he asked her what happened between them during the night.

He was uncomfortable that she was more sexually experienced than him, and he worried that he might not be able to please her.

When she came out of the bathroom, he was sitting up naked on the bed. She turned the lights out as she walked in, and tried to force herself on him, but he resisted and insisted that he put on the condom first.

"I don't want to use condoms," she protested. "I just want it to feel natural."

He reached for a condom and opened it, but he wasn't aroused anymore, so he didn't try to put it on. He was using the condom as a form of threat to chase her away from him.

She got annoyed at his insistence that they use a condom. She turned her back to him and began typing something on her cellphone. Why she had her cellphone in her hand while attempting to have sexual intercourse was a strange thing in itself. But this didn't seem to bother Gideon at all; he was now more concerned about getting her to leave.

"Who are you texting?" he asked.

"Just my friends," she mumbled, and continued typing.

He lay in the bed flat on his back staring at the ceiling. His right arm was over his face, and his left arm on his crotch. He was thinking what he might do to make her leave. He didn't see her coming towards him. She hurried into the bed, climbed on top of him, and immediately started gyrating her body on him, trying to get him aroused once more. He tried to resist her by sitting up, but she held him down, forcing his arms behind his head, and continued twisting and turning – writhing her body on top of him. It worked. He was now worked up and ready to enter her, but she didn't know that.

He felt the moistness from her vagina as she twerked and gyrated – rubbing her clitoris against his cock. Her pale skin glowed in the dark. He thought her eyes were blue when he'd seen them in the mirror, but now they look dark and shiny, like a luminous purple glowing in the dark.

She moaned and started to talk dirty to him. "You like that, don't you baby?! You know you want it. You want to fuck my little pussy, huh?! It's all yours baby. I want to feel your cock inside me. I want you to come inside my little pussy. Yes baby, you like that, don't you!"

She gyrated on him and carried on like this for about a minute and a half. She felt him getting harder and longer, and she grabbed his cock and tried to position herself to mount it. Suddenly he ejaculated into her hand and onto her crotch. She felt him vibrating in her hand; she looked down and saw the sperm glowing on her hand.

"Oh my gosh! Did you come?!" she exclaimed.

"Yes, I did," Gideon said.

"Why didn't you tell me you were going to come?" she said, getting off of him. She scornfully walked to the bathroom, trying not to let the sperm drip from her clitoris onto the floor.

She was in the bathroom for a little while, cleaning the sperm from her hand and pubic area. Gideon took this opportunity to clean himself as well and put his clothes on. She returned from the bathroom a few minutes later, still naked. When she saw that he was already dressed, she was even more disappointed.

She looked at him, then turned her back to him and began messing with her cellphone once again.

"I'm sorry I came so fast. I didn't want to, but I haven't had sex in a while," Gideon told her, sitting up relaxed on the bed.

With her back still turned to him, she said, "You're fine; I just wish you had told me that you were going to come."

The disappointment could be felt like rain drops on his skin. An eerie moment of perpetual silence passed between them. She was disappointed because she didn't react fast enough; she had allowed him to ejaculate before penetrating her. He was disappointed because he didn't know this girl, and probably would never see her again. He could care less what she thought of him after the short and unusual intercourse. But it troubled him, because she almost had him: she would've let him ejaculate inside her.

He was satisfied, and she wasn't, but that was not his fault. She could've had him inside her in the first place if she had allowed him to wear the condom. But instead, she tried to overpower him, to get him to the point of no return, where he'd be too hot and bothered to refuse her.

She walked close to him – still fiddling with her cellphone. She forced herself onto his lap, and just sat there – saying nothing and paying him no attention. She waited for his reaction, for his hands to caress her naked body; this would mean that he was ready to go again, and this time she would make it right. She would make sure that he penetrated her and ejaculated inside her, no matter how short the intercourse.

She inched her body closer to him; if she turned and faced him, her vagina would be on his face. She wanted him to know that she wasn't done yet; she wanted to be satisfied. But he was behind her being cautious, trying not to look too lustful at her naked body, for fear he might get aroused once more; for by this point, he was probably thinking that she must have some unknown motive up her sleeve, something sinister. Why did she so desperately want to have a stranger's essence inside her?

He didn't want to touch her. Instead, he reacted in the most unpleasant way: behind her back, he carefully leaned away from her, planting both his arms on the bed behind him, as if cuffing them behind his back. *"I'm not touching you; we're not going to do this,"* he said to himself. *"Please Lord, just let her give up or stop.* She had her cellphone in her hand and was looking at the screen. She didn't notice his reaction, because her back was turned to him.

After seeing how desperate she was to have his sperm, he became curious, and he was glad that he hadn't penetrated her.

Shadow People

She was trying to get him aroused once more, and even though she managed to do so, he wouldn't budge. After several minutes, she went back into the bathroom once more, at which point, her cellphone rang. The person on the other end seemed to be asking her for directions to where she was. She had the water running, but Gideon could hear some of what they were saying. She tried to explain to the person on the other end that nothing had happened between them, that they really hadn't had sex.

"We did, but not really."

"What do you mean?"

"It just didn't work out."

"What do you mean, it didn't work out? Did you have sex or not?"

"Yes, but he came too fast."

"So that's good, that's exactly what you want!"

"No, it's not like that. Nothing happened."

"What do you mean nothing happened? I don't understand what you're saying. You had sex, right?"

"Yes, but..."

"But what?"

"Nothing happened!"

"What? I don't understand!"

"It's complicated. I'll explain it to you later."

"Where are you at?"

"I'm in his apartment."

"What's his address? We're coming there now."

"No, don't. I'm about to leave."

"It doesn't matter. Where are you at?"

"I told you, nothing happened!"

"What's the address?"

"I don't know."

"So, ask him!"

"It's the green and yellow building behind Kroger, I think it's called college something. But it doesn't matter because nothing happened and I'm about to leave now."

"College Suites! I know where that is. We're coming right now."

"Oh my gosh, I told you..." The person on the other end hung up.

She set the cellphone on the dresser and began tidying herself up.

"Who was that?" Gideon asked.

"Just my friends," she replied.

Her cellphone kept beeping and vibrating with messages, but she ignored it and continued putting her clothes on, until it rang once again. She answered

"Hello!" she said, rushing into the bathroom once more, and closing the door behind her.

"What's the code to get in through the gate?"

"What? Where are you?"

"We're in the parking lot by the gate," the person said, laughing.

"What! How did you get here so fast? Were you following me?"

"Ha ha ha ha ha!" The menacing laughter could be heard even over the noise from the flushing of the toilet.

"Maybe! When you said the green and yellow building behind Kroger, we were close by."

"You shouldn't have come. I'm leaving now."

"What building are you at?"

"I don't know."

"Ask him what building. What's his apartment number?"

"I don't know; I think it's 500 and something. I don't know his apartment number."

"So, ask him, we're coming in."

"No, don't come. I've already told you, nothing happened!"

"What's the apartment number?"

"You're not listening to me. Nothing happened!"

"What's the number?"

"Ok, fine. I'm leaving now. I'll meet you in the parking lot. Where are you parked?"

"No, just tell me his apartment number, and we'll come in!"

She ended the call, and rushed from the bathroom with her things, and then she rushed back into the bathroom to brush her hair and put on more makeup. She dressed quickly and was ready to leave. Gideon walked with her through the living room, opened the door for her, said goodbye, and then quickly shut the door behind her. If there had been a bolt on the lock, he would've bolted the door.

"Who was she talking to, and why did they want to come into my apartment?" he thought. He was a bit concerned by this, because he didn't know who these people were.

"Thank God I didn't have sex with her," he said to himself.

Even more bizarre, the person she spoke with wanted to make sure that she had sex with him. Otherwise, according to the conversation he overheard, it would be unnecessary for them to come to the apartment. She told them not to come, because they didn't actually have sex: it was complicated. But they wouldn't listen; they didn't believe her.

What would've happened to him if they had sex? Gideon was quite troubled by this. They did engage in sexual intercourse, but there was no penetration involved; he ejaculated before she was able to mount him; which she seemed quite upset about.

What was her goal besides having sex? Why were her friends so determined to meet with her at his apartment?

Remembering that he still hadn't done grocery shopping as yet, for he was sidetracked by her earlier in the Kroger parking lot. He took a bath before contemplating going back to the store.

He condemns himself after considering everything that could've happened to him: he could've been robbed and killed. What if her plan had worked? What could she have intended to happen to him? He was grateful that her plan didn't work. He then said a short prayer before leaving to go to the store.

It has been about 30 minutes since she left, but when he went outside, Nikki was still in her Jeep with the engine running - and pulled up next to his vehicle. She was talking to someone in the parking lot who was also parked nearby; she was pointing in the direction of his vehicle, but she seemed uncertain which of the cars were his. She was shocked when she saw him coming and waving at her.

"Hey, you're still here?" he asked her, but she didn't reply to him. Instead, she ignored him and drove away. Gideon supposed that she was still upset with him, but he also took this to be a warning: there were several persons in a vehicle nearby; they were leaning back and watching him as he was walking to his car. Whoever they were, they didn't want to be seen. They also drove a Cherokee Jeep, a sparkling black one that looked like it had just been washed and waxed. The windows were tinted black; he couldn't really see inside the vehicle. In fact, it was so dark that the people inside looked like shadows with eyes that moved about in the dark. Even though it was still light out, he just couldn't quite make them out.

Gideon stopped for a moment to gaze into the vehicle: several pairs of fiery oval rings (that could've been eyes) reflected on the tinted windows. They were crisscrossing and moving about in unusual patterns, which made him believe that whosoever was inside the vehicle looking at him, they weren't human. He wanted to confront them, but he was too afraid. He immediately got into his vehicle and drove away.

"Are they car thieves?" was the first thought that came to mind. "But then again, they don't seem human. They were working together with that girl."

When Gideon returned from the grocery store, he realized that he didn't have Nikki's phone number in his phone. He wanted to call her and ask her about the men who kept calling her: Who were they? What did they want? Were those her friends outside in the parking lot? He asked for her phone number when they were together in the parking lot, but she never gave her phone number to him. Instead, she had insisted on following him back to his residence.

The only thing he knew about her was that her name was Nikki, which wasn't even her real name. When he checked her identification earlier, he jokingly told her that her ID was fake. But then he paid no attention to the fact that she'd gotten angry at him for saying this; for she had so willingly flashed her identification at his face. He only wanted to verify her age, and since she was exactly 18; he didn't bother to confirm that it was her picture on the ID card. He should've paid attention to the other details as well - her real name, the color of her eyes, and the color of her hair.

Gideon searched his phone for the pictures he had taken earlier, but there was just one photo of her left in his phone; which made him feel uneasy, because he noticed something strange about her eyes; they were dark and hollow. This made her look like a soulless being.

He got up at once to make sure that all the windows and doors were closed, because he got scared remembering the black Cherokee jeep that parked next to him outside. He wondered whether they were still out there in the parking lot. They were there when he left to go shopping. However, when he returned, he parked on the opposite side of the building.

She played the innocent coquette, while her friends were outside waiting for her - to do who knows what to her victims. He locked himself in his bedroom and put some furniture behind the door; then he began praying once more. He was really spooked. His mind began racing; he couldn't really concentrate on what he was praying about.

Gideon had seen two dark figures in the front seat of the vehicle; these figures seemed to be leaning back. There were several figures in the back seat of the vehicle that were moving about suspiciously, like they were anxious to see him. He couldn't see their bodies; he only saw what looked like pairs of eyes floating about in the dark.

"Maybe they were body snatchers, like changelings who wanted to replace me?"

He also thought of the possibility that this girl may've been a demon herself, but that she wore a human body, and that is why she didn't care about being protected.

"I'm going crazy," he said to himself, wrapping himself with the sheets. But the thought of it terrified him. He was under the covers thinking about her: *"Maybe she's part of an organized group that practiced the dark arts – witchcraft, satanic rituals, and other things like that. Maybe that's why she wanted to get pregnant: to use the baby for a sacrifice? But that would not explain why the other guys had been there. What did they want? Why did they come?"*

The thing that puzzled him the most was that he had had to ask her several times to come into the apartment. Every time he opened the door for her, she would not go in until she had been invited in. She did not enter the apartment when he first opened the door; he had gone in ahead of her, and when he turned to look for her, she was by the door looking away. He had watched as the door began closing in her face. He had to go back, open the door and ask her to come in. The same thing happened again when he had opened the door to his bedroom. She did not go in until after he asked her to come in.

Gideon didn't know what to make of this whole situation, because it was rather strange to him, especially because he couldn't explain why those men were waiting outside.

Gideon thought of the possibility that she may have had something inside her vagina. He just couldn't put the pieces together, but he was glad to know that he hadn't penetrated her.

His untimely ejaculation saved him. What would've happened had he penetrated and ejaculated inside her?

She was very attractive, but who in their right mind meets a stranger on the street and insists on having sex with them for the first time without wearing protection.

Desperation makes a man perform incredible feats, but it also makes him into an easy target. The fool sees her outer beauty and falls in love at first sight. But if he was vigilant, he would've seen that she was a devil in disguise. He had taken no notice of her strange behavior - her walking back and forth from her vehicle to the pump, and how she'd placed the nozzle inside the tank before entering her credentials. She wasn't there to get gas; she was there to seduce him. She saw him as an easy target, which is why she carried this air of naïveté about her: to make him rue the day, if he hadn't approached and talked to her.

It's funny how men think that they're in charge; they believe that they are the ones running things, when women are the ones controlling everything. Women have been glorified since their beginning. She's been endowed with beauty and affection, and her beauty is the curse of men. She convinces him, as Eve convinced Adam, to eat of her forbidden fruits, and then, she binds him to her Garden of Eden. She becomes his treasure trove, to which he bestows all his valuables. She is his pride and joy. Without her, that man is nothing.

Some women complain that they are not equal to men, that they are of lesser value and have less rights. Wrong! It is because of women that men grow their appetite: to impress her. The king wants to conquer the world and give it to his woman. He sacrificed the fate of his entire kingdom to please her; and yet, when she became accustomed to his courtiers, she complained to them, saying that she's not being treated well, and that she lives like a peasant; even while his entire kingdom is at her feet. She just cannot be satisfied. She always wants more. But the way that she dances pleases the mad king. He grants her this one wish:

"What do you desire, my dear?" asked the king.

"Your prisoner's head!" she exclaimed.

And just like that, John the Baptist's head was severed and placed on a platter for her.

One kiss from her lips, and, in an instant, the strongman became weak. She lulled him to sleep and then she asked someone to shave his head. When he awoke, realizing he had no dignity left; for, with his shaved head, he could no longer call on the strength that he once knew. He gave in; and the Philistines came and captured him.

She's lauded by her beauty, idolized for her allure. But she's often very ugly on the inside; and she's much too glorified to see this. Men kill one another to get a taste of her booty, that luscious piece of land thatched between her thighs, like a river that flows with milk and honey. Even the noblest travelers lose their way when they see her dancing seductively under the brazen sun. The wine in the glass is sour; but yet, mysteriously, a lively rhythm they feel.

Oh, how sweet and delicate her misery, too subtle to ignore. Charged with sexual fantasies, men shall have their desires satisfied. Their naked eyes would never see the sinister powers that lie dormant beneath her flesh. They would never imagine the dangers of coalescing with these untethered souls.

Men and women unknowingly do this to each other all the time: Gideon didn't know that he was being hypnotized. His spirit was now entwined with hers. God forbids that he should dance this soulless dance with an advocate of the devil.

"But how was I to know this?" he asked himself, dreaming. "This stranger came to my apartment in the middle of the night and exposed herself to me. It was the perfect chance for me, because I haven't had sex in many years, although I got lucky the night before."

"This beautiful and lovely teenage girl: it was guaranteed sexual intercourse. Who would miss out on that? I just didn't know she'd be like this and take the part of me that I cannot get back: my God-given essence."

Using her powers to manipulate him, this creature would invade his mind and capture him. She would wield his vitality like a sword, cutting through provinces, leaving behind hearts and minds aching - brothers, sister, and next of kin, their heads thick with blood, their hearts heavy and hardened. Once this evil entity enters the soul, he will never be the same again; he would become her indentured servant.

She masquerades as beauty in the middle of the night; skimpily dressed, her skin glowing in the dark. She looks lovely on the outside, but on the inside, she is full of dead men's bones. If only his eyes could see beyond this flesh, he would notice this demonic presence in front of him; ready, anxiously waiting to drag him into hell and feast on his flesh.

Men, we are vulnerable creatures you know, we are susceptible to spirits of the higher and lower realms. These spirit beings can interact with us through our emotions. They can manipulate and influence us through our thoughts. Most times, we are at the mercy of our family members and friends and the people we come in contact with on a daily basis - how they treat us: what they say, what they do, and what they think about us, affect our emotional wellbeing.

Thoughts are born of the spirit, the energy that surrounds us. When we dream, we enter the thought world, where entities can attach themselves to us through our subconscious mind. The subconscious mind is the body, which is the way we feel, see, and do things. Entities who enter our thought world have the ability to strengthen or weaken our emotions, and they can manipulate and influence us to do things based on this energy field around us. This is what Jesus meant when he said, "where the corpse is, there the vultures will gather."

We can't see the spirit realm, but they can see us. They intend to use our bodies (our corpse) for sensual pleasures; they do not have physical bodies of their own. The vultures know when we are weak; for they are more advanced than us. They understand on a visceral level what sort of emotional experiences we're having. If our environment is in emotional chaos, they will know that we are weak and vulnerable. However, if we are not fearful or worried, our ethereal body will be impenetrable; for we're united - body, mind, and spirit. The people we have in our circle, must also hold us in high regards; otherwise, they will bring harm to us by having bad thoughts about us.

Nikki came to him again after midnight. There was a knock at the door of his apartment; Gideon woke up startled. He waited to be sure that that is what he was hearing.

"Bum, bum, bum, bum, bum, bum," the knocking continued.

He rushed out of bed without checking to see what time it was.

"Who's it?" He stood behind the door and shouted.

"It's me, Ikkin!" The creature said revealing its real name, but Gideon feeling a little groggy thought he heard her say Nikki, so he opened the door.

She stood in the doorway looking in at him and waiting for him to say something. But instead, he stood in the doorway amazed - just gazing at her naked body. He'd never known her to be so beautiful, nor has he seen anyone as beautiful as her before.

"May I come in? She asks finally.

"Yes, come in," he said, gesturing to her.

As soon as she walks in, she starts caressing on him without giving him time to close the door. As the door slammed itself shut behind them, she let go of him and waited for him to get undressed. He walks into the bedroom ahead of her as he starts getting undressed. First, he took his shirt off, then he noticed her standing outside the bedroom door and looking at him, waiting to be invited in. It was the same scenes all over again.

"Come in," he told her once more.

As soon as she walked in, she pushed him onto the bed, and hurriedly pulled his pants off his legs. She then climbs on top of him and immediately begins to ride him. The bed started rattling and making squeaking sounds as she gyrated her body on top of him, making mournful sounds as she rode him faster and harder.

She let out a soft but high-pitched squeamish mourn, and then in came these shadowy figures, more than a hundred of them rushed into the room. He felt stifled as the room got darker, and the air became clammy.

Gideon didn't as yet notice the dark figures encircling his bed, because they were so dark that he couldn't see them. However, he could feel something strange happening around him.

She rode him slowly, and then faster and faster. The feeling was so intense. Suddenly, the room became like utter blackness, and he could no longer feel his arms and legs. The creatures were holding him down on the bed; he saw long white teeths grinning - with many pairs of eyes glowing in the dark. He heard them laughing, they sound like children, more than a hundred of them.

She rode him harder and faster, making mournful sounds and shaking the bed. He wanted her to stop; he begged for her to stop. "Get off of me!" he shouted. But no words came out of his mouth, instead, the feeling became more intense. He felt himself sinking deeper and deeper in the bed; he was going down into utter blackness; the creatures were laughing, and the smell of rotten flesh seemed to be burning all around him.

She starts to vibrate vigorously on top of him. He tried to move, but he was paralyzed, and he couldn't hear himself shouting. She then leaned into him, and that ugly demonic presence revealed itself fully. A white-haired creature with a huge chunk missing from its head was sitting on top of him; it was holding him down and looking at him. It had a skeletal body with rotten flesh barely hanging from its bones; he could see right through it, even through its head.

She sat on top of him – waiting, as they went deeper into the abyss. He tried to scream - over and over again. He could hear himself shouting, but he couldn't move. "Jesus, help me please!" he said aloud, but the words wouldn't come out. He was going down into this other realm with this creature on top of him.

Gazing up at this creature sitting on his pelvis, he tried to look away, but he couldn't move his head. He then closed his eyes and said from within, "Jesus ...," and before he could finish what he was about to say, the creatures flung themselves away from him. Then he awoke and realized that it was just a dream.

He got out of bed immediately and turned on the lights, grabbed his Bible, knelt down, and began to pray. When he finished praying, he looked at the time; it was 3:33 am. He raised his right hand to touch his forehead, then down to his belly, raised it again to touch his left shoulder, and then over to his right shoulder, then he clasped his hands into his chest and said, "Amen."

The Coming War

Gideon woke up the next morning feeling tired, like he could sleep for another 6 hours. While he was in the shower getting ready, he thought about the dream that he'd had, and how this girl came back to him in the middle of the night. He believed the dream was trying to reveal something to him: that this girl may've been under the influence of evil, and that she and her friends were going to do something wicked to him.

He thought deeply about these possibilities: Nikki's role was to lure him by having sex with him and inflict damage to him in some way during sexual intercourse; after which, the entities, her friends on the outside, would come in to do the rest.

During sexual intercourse, particularly at the point of ejaculation, the pineal gland, the pathway to the soul life opens. Entities are inter-sexed, which means that they can take on the role of both male and female partners.

Gideon being Christian, he must subject himself only to the light, and he is bound by spiritual contract to keep a clean conscience before God. Whenever Christians break this contract, they become subjects of the spirit realm. The spirit beings can use their bodies for physical experiences.

This dark entity that he had encountered was an alien as well. She is from the planet Evol, which is the opposite of the beings of pure light who came from the planet Lemone. She too wanted to collect his essence; that is why she wanted to be penetrated without him putting on a condom first. However, lucky for him, her plans fell through, because according to the beings of pure light, she would've corrupted his soul and the light in him would die, which explains why the other dark entities were with her. She wanted to penetrate his soul life and corrupt his light, and then the spirits who came with her would possess him. They would take over his soul: he would be the same physically, but not in spirit; he would become like a wicked person.

Gideon didn't know this, but these entities of light and entities of darkness have been fighting for many generations. The beings of light made this known to him: that there is a great war in the heavens between the entities of light and the entities of darkness.

"She was one of the seven sisters of darkness who came to you. They travel together many of them, but very lucky for you and for us that she cannot capture you, because if she captures your soul life, many harms will come to us for mating with you."

"So why wasn't I able to see that she was a dark entity?" Gideon asks.

"She is one of seven sisters of darkness that came from planet Evol. We are seven sisters of light from planet Lemone, our people are at war with each other. This war has not yet come but will happen very soon."

"I'm confused. What do you mean by saying that you are at war with each other, but that the war has not happened yet?"

"You cannot know her because very deceptive spirit. She appears like a normal person, but very dark inside."

"Many thousands of years ago, Marah, one of the seven sisters of darkness, came to your planet, and she corrupted many souls of men. Men's souls become dark and kill each other."

"I saw your sister Attannania in my vision; I saw her people and how she was raised. But then there was a great war on your planet, and many people died. Is this the same war you speak about?"

"Yes. We can see many thousands of years into the future. My sister Attannania gave you gift, so you can also see future as well."

In this vision, Gideon saw their father and 12 leading men at table. "You are my most prized possession," said the father, "you are more loved than the angels. I offer to you: my daughters, he said, pointing at them. "They are the seven sisters of light. They will come to you, although you may not know them; they will open your eyes."

"This is what we must do for each other: we must sacrifice. Too many people have become materialized. If Darkness reclaims what was once hers, the universe will die. For out of this void, the universe was created. But imagine for a moment that the souls of men should live in perpetual torment."

"Thus far, nothing that man has created or discovered can withstand the extreme temperatures of the sun, and the sun is the least extreme of them all. The universe will die if man becomes thickened with darkness."

"You see this ring?" said her father, raising his right hand towards his face: a big purple stone glistened on his fourth finger; it glowed with light, as if it contained the powers of the entire universe. And the men at the table all bowed their heads. Then suddenly, Gideon's body seized up, and he was caught in a daze staring at the ring.

"Summon the dragon," her father said, and the other twelve men seated at the table raised their fists. They all had different color stones on their fourth fingers: one had a blue stone, another had a red stone, another had a green stone, another had a yellow stone, another had a white stone, another had a black stone, and six of them had different color stones that he didn't recognize; for they were colors that he had not yet seen. And one of the six had a stone that was transparent, for he couldn't see its color. They all at once uttered a name, but the name they uttered were different, so that it may complete the one name. For no man cannot say this name alone; for there were twelve voices in one; and the creature would not have come."

Then shone forth a different color light from each of their rings, and the lights became as liquid encircling the table above their heads; it flowed mysteriously and coagulated, and then a creature emerged and expanded. It was a giant serpent-like creature with wings. It floated about in the air, and snaked its body towards Gideon's face, as if to frighten him, but Gideon didn't move, because he couldn't move. The creature stared directly into his eyes, and without using words, the creature said to him, "we've been waiting for the past two thousand years, and now you have come."

Gideon was staring into the eyes of a dragon.

There is a certain consciousness attached to the idea that aliens are here to take over our planet; and what if they're really here?

What most people don't realize is that illuminated beings, aliens, angels, and demons are truly among us. Your friend, the police, even your politician could be one of them and you wouldn't know it. What if they look just like us? What do they want from us? Why did they come here? How will the things they do impact or influence us? How will they treat us?

We're living in their new world now, though we just can't see it yet. How else would you explain everything that's going on?

The lukewarm people of society are their greatest allies. Their alien desires have put us in unfavorable circumstances; and even as they reveal themselves to us, we still don't know who they are. The aliens were already here; they are among us.

www.the-crazy-author.com